Happy

PARANOIA IN THE LAUNDERETTE

PARANOIA IN THE LAUNDERETTE

bruce robinson

BLOOMSBURY

First published by Bloomsbury Publishing Plc 1998

Copyright © Bruce Robinson 1998

The moral right of the author has been asserted

Bloomsbury Publishing Plc, 38 Soho Square,
London W1V 5DF

A CIP catalogue is available from the British Library

ISBN 0 7475 4243 0

10 9 8 7 6 5 4 3 2 1

Typeset by Hewer Text Limited, Edinburgh

Printed by St Edmundsbury Press, Suffolk

I had been carrying a carving knife around with me for three weeks due to an irrational fear of being murdered. I couldn't sleep at night. As soon as I got into bed I started seeing killers – usually a nose or a toecap of a killer's boot disappearing round the bedroom door. These killers were always on the move. One night I said, 'Oy,' as I caught sight of a killer's top-hat coming in at knee-height at the end of the bed. I started to sleep in an upright position with the light on. But my vigilance made them crafty and since then they kept low-profile in the hall, crawling around on their hands and knees or coming in at a stoop to avoid being seen . . .

I became particularly frightened of a man I called the Beetle. He wore a black cloak, a

1

top-hat, and appeared the instant I shut my eyes to sleep. The Beetle was a poisoner and knife man. His smile was dreadful, and coupled with his cloak and toecaps he kept me awake for a week. Three or four times a night I'd spot him moseying around behind the crack in the door and I'd have to get up and creep along the corridor between the kitchen and the living room looking for him behind the sofa and in the airing cupboard. I also looked for him under the bed in case he'd slipped in while I was looking in the refrigerator. I was so convinced of his presence I even looked for him in the oven, expecting to find him crouched and ready to spring out as I opened the door . . .

Because of the Beetle I started carrying the carving knife. This fear that I would be murdered began with my decision to write a series of plays for the television set called *Decades of Death*. The nature of the project necessitated research into heinous Victorian criminals and I had unwittingly familiarised myself with all the famous hackers, dosers and severers of the nineteenth century. My bedroom was piled with volumes about brutes. I had photographs of mass-murderers pinned to the wall. I had a book published in 1929 with over two hundred examples of the 'Criminal Stare'. There were faces in here that would have frightened Crippen. Thousands of warped noses were between its covers, and so were glassy eyeballs and hare-lips. And worst of them all, opposite page 117, the Bearded Pole with the bow tie. This wall-eyed short-arse was known as Long Ear. He was the terrible Jewish plumber who had hacked a Frenchman's head off. After disposing of limbs down sewers he found himself at a loss as to what he should do with the head. Finally, by utilising his gas-fired crucible, he filled the mouth and ears with molten lead, and slung it in a river . . .

This head played on my mind. I found it impossible to get to sleep at night without thinking of the Head. I started plugging my ears and kept my mouth shut. But thoughts of the Head stayed with me and I became anxious in case the cotton wool should give the Beetle an advantage in his creepings. I read other cases to take my mind off it . . .

There was a maniac in North London called The Hendon Ogre, who had boiled the arsenic out of fly-papers and introduced the result into his lodger's broth. Knowledge of this had no effect on the Frenchman's Head. Lying awake at night I continued to think of the Frenchman's Head while at the same time being convinced that somebody was introducing arsenic into my diet. I developed symptoms. My legs went stiff and I sat up for hours looking at my finger-nails for *signs*. Both arms were perpetually out in an enthusiastic fascist salute. In the mornings I inspected grapefruit and milk-bottle tops looking for evidence of interference with syringes. I suspected everybody and began to interpret even the most trivial events as something that would later be used as a vital clue in detection of my assassin. If the telephone rang, I would look at my watch and say, 'It was six-thirty when the telephone rang that fateful evening. How could anybody have known at that time how important that telephone call was to become?' If it was a wrong number, I would say, 'What appeared to be a wrong number, turned out (as the facts will illustrate), to be one of the first seemingly trivial events that led up to this monstrous crime.'

It was about four o'clock when the telephone rang. I was in bed with a pot of tea and some Garibaldi biscuits preparing to go in for some afternoon recoupment. Since the Beetle had come into my life my face had become puffy through lack of sleep and I was beginning to show signs of the nights I'd spent upright with my arms out.

I looked at my watch. I said, 'It was four minutes past four when the telephone rang.' I decided not to answer it and it stopped. A minute later it started again. At seven minutes past four it was still ringing and I was forced to get out of bed and answer it . . .

'Hello,' I said.

My 'Literary Agent' was on the line.

'Why haven't you been answering the telephone?'

'I thought you were a wrong number.'

'Well, listen,' she said, 'I've just had a very excited man on the phone.'

'Have you?'

'He's read your treatment for *Decades of Death*, and is very excited by your ideas. It's of the utmost importance he sees you to-night at six o'clock.'

I looked at my watch and told her it was already ten minutes past four and that I was about to go to sleep in preparation for being up all night. She agreed with me about the time but said the man was going to New York and that it was imperative that I saw him before he left.

'Why is it imperative that I see him before he leaves?'

'Because he's *Harvey Humphries.*'

'Harvey Humphries? Who is he?'

'Head of Scripts.'

'Couldn't I see him when he gets back from New York? I haven't been sleeping well recently.'

'That's quite impossible. The arrangement has been made for tonight at six, and you'll have to go.'

'That's one hour forty-seven minutes,' I said.

'Wear a suit,' she said.

'I don't have any suits.'

'Well, wear a clean shirt, then?'

'All my shirts are dirty.'

She put a hand over the receiver and spoke to somebody else before she came back.

'Then you'll have to go to the launderette, won't you?'

She put the phone down on my reply.

I walked into the bedroom feeling pressurised and looking at the address I'd written on the back of a cigarette packet: 'Harvey Humphries, 100, Humbolt Mews.'

I had sat in every Head of Scripts department in London listening to these twats full of arugula and white wine, but I'd never heard of this man Harvey Humphries or his Humbolt Mews address. Harvey Humphries of Humbolt Mews? I didn't like the sound of it. Though the name seemed innocent enough, there was something about it that jarred. I thought for a minute it was the Harvey/Humphries/Humbolt bit that was worrying me, but I had a friend called Garry Gordon who lived in Garrick Street, and he never caused me any problem. It was something stronger than just a repetition of the H – it was more a sensation of having heard the name Harvey Humphries before in some unsavoury context . . .

Sitting on the edge of the bed I sank a mouthful of tea. It went down my throat like a finger. Suddenly I remembered where I'd heard the name Harvey Humphries and I rose to my feet in time to see my eyes widen into the mirror opposite . . .

'Harvey,' I whispered. It was the Harvey.

Harvey was the middle name of Dr Hawley Harvey Crippen, the myopic Yank who'd spent all night in the basement of 39, Hilldrop Crescent, N5, separating his wife.

He done her in lime. My mind raced.

Crippen had come from America. Harvey Humphries was going to America within hours of completing his business with me? My reflection buckled at the horrifying idea that had just got in behind it.

9

Was Humphries related to Crippen?

Far-fetched as it might sound to others, it was not impossible. Within a minute I was convinced of it. Surely it was more than coincidence that a man going to America in the morning should be excited by a title like *Decades of Death*, and have the middle name of one of the most famous killers of the lot? Facts like that were beyond the realm of coincidence . . .

I went into the kitchen for my carving knife considering the facts. Fact one was the way my agent had spoken to me. It was quite out of character for her to be officious and demanding and why, I asked myself, had she suddenly taken an interest in my laundry? I'd been all over London in dirty shirts without discussing them with her over the telephone. Most of her clients looked like gardeners or men on the run, and it bothered me that a woman who habitually associated with unkempt depressives should suddenly start wanting to get them all into suits. It didn't add up. No, it didn't add up at all. It was almost as though she were trying to set something up for me to walk into. Like a trap. And, in fact, how was I to know that it was really my agent who called? It could have been anybody with a handkerchief over the mouth. It was the oldest trick in the book . . .

I got on the phone immediately and asked the secretary to hand Clair across. She said Clair had been out of the office all day, and anyway, she was only a temporary and wouldn't really know her if she saw her. I described my agent in detail and the girl said she'd have been certain to have spotted anyone with huge earlobes and a blue/grey rinse on a slightly balding head, and that she was sorry but she could be of no further assistance . . .

'Do you know Harvey Humphries?' I said.

'No,' she said.

I went back into the bedroom trying to be rational. If she wasn't in the office, she must have telephoned from home. That was quite clear. But as I didn't have her private number I wasn't going to be able to call her back.

Now then, where did that get me?

I knew at once that I was going to have to trust that it was she who called, and that she'd done it without malice. After all she had no reason for wishing me harmed. It probably never crossed her mind that she was sending one of her clients to see a man related to a murderer. Only a highly suspicious paranoid cynic, or someone like me, would have ever caught on to the possibility of Harvey Humphries being Hawley Harvey Crippen's son . . .

In an effort to get my mind off Humphries' relative, I sank to the floor to have a look at my wardrobe. I kept it in a black polythene bag in the corner. Most of the items in here hadn't come out since they'd first gone in last Christmas. There were socks, shirts, pants, and a bow tie and several other things people had given me. Everything but the bow tie was filthy and even that stank. I selected the least soiled shirt, pants, and a couple of socks and took them into the kitchen. After a quick thrash in the sink I squeezed them out and stuck them in the oven. This was the only way for a fast dry. A pair of socks usually takes between fifteen and twenty minutes on regulo 9. Five minutes less for the pants, and the shirt should have ideally gone in later on regulo 4 or 5. But I was in a hurry and didn't have time for complicated domestic equations . . .

At four-thirty I got into the bath with my carving knife. I was too tense to bathe and lay on my back squirting water out of a hypodermic syringe. Nerves were getting the better of me. No matter how I tried I

13

couldn't prevent myself from indulging in visions of Humphries in his cellar. I put him down for a precise little bloke with glasses like the end of tonic-water bottles. Transparent eyebrows and manicured nails. It made me shudder.

I brought my hypodermic needle up through the water and aimed a stream at an empty shampoo bottle. Once I'd knocked it into the bath I strafed it unmercifully while considering my strategy. I would refuse to sit down, refuse all drinks and cigarettes. The interview would be conducted standing up. If he went out of the room I would go with him. I would have a pretext for everything. I might even devise a circumstance to get my carving knife out over his coffee table.

But even on the thought I realised the fragility of my defence. It seemed foolish to believe I could put the wind up a man I had never met who had already put the wind up me simply because his mother had decided to call him Harvey . . .

By the time I got out of the bath I was glossy with anxiety. Words like 'blood' and 'lime' kept crossing my mind. I started imagining headlines.

'THE HUMBOLT CASE,' I suddenly said out loud.

The Humbolt case? It sounded convincing. I was just getting into it when a stench of burning garbage rooted me to the spot. I opened the bathroom door and the hall was full of smoke. For an instant I thought the house was on fire and I set off towards the front door shouting, 'Fire, Fire.' In sudden realisation I then turned rapidly on a foot and plunged towards the kitchen shouting, 'Not the Socks. Not the Socks.'

Bursting in I got the oven open but was beaten back by an explosion of heat that must have taken my eyelashes off. My shirt was on fire. I could clearly see the glow of its

15

collar through the dense combination of nylon vapour and atomised dripping. I got the gas off, adjusted breathing, and shoved my head back into the pall of roasted clothes. The shirt was so thoroughly dried out it was in flames as far down as the shoulder blades. The pants had already gone up, and one sock had practically disintegrated. There was nothing left of it but a smouldering woollen tube with ash falling off . . .

I sank to the lino in panic. Wild ideas of socks going under the grill and arriving at 100, Humbolt Mews in a clean but saturated shirt momentarily passed through my mind. But it was five minutes to five and too late to prepare other garments. The reality of the situation was in the corner of my bedroom in the black polythene sack. The situation was hopeless, and I knew it. I was without shirt, pantless, and had nothing clean in the house except a woollen tube.

It hung on the end of my carving knife for a moment and went out. The other sock came out of the oven as hard as crackling. For some mysterious reason it hadn't burnt but been fired, like a terracotta pot. Part of its toe was taken off, but the bulk had survived and was clearly wearable. My spirits rose a little. Though it was almost a 'boot' in its own right, I discovered that with a shoe laced around it, the tube looked perfectly normal. But I had to stand still. As soon as I began to walk it sprang out and started ascending the shin. It looked like a spat. If I was going to be following a stranger around his house with a knife, this thing would be of no use to me whatsoever. Somehow, I was going to have to get hold of someone's clean clothes.

My mind went blank.

I had been living alone too long and the only person I could think of with clean clothes was my mother. My only remote and groundless hope was that I had missed something in my wardrobe, and so for the second time in an hour I went back into my polythene bag.

It was worse than I remembered. Its contents seemed to have deteriorated in the last half-hour. There was nothing. My choice was reduced to the unlaunderable (and if the word doesn't exist, then neither did this pile in front of me). These clothes were worse than filthy. You could have taken most of them into a garden and dug them in around the roses. These clothes were refuse. As I mined the pile those prophetic words from my agent's lips came back . . .

'You'll have to go to the launderette then, won't you?'

It was true. There was nothing I could do with this lot on my own. I was going to have to go to the launderette . . .

The reality of it horrified me. The launderette was not a place for me, a man so sensitive I had never even bought a toilet roll. I got toilet rolls through the kindness of friends. I could never walk into a chemist's shop cold-bloodedly demanding to know where they kept their toilet rolls. In my opinion we'd all be better off if toilet rolls were on prescription only. There would of course be a certain amount of invonveni-ence for both the doctors and the public, but as I pointed out in my letter to the *Lancet*, the gains would far outweigh the monthly visit to the out-patients'. If the system I outlined had been introduced I think there would be a good chance to get the laundries into the National Health as well. In that way one's bundle could be dealt with by experienced handlers who have training and are immune to shock.

Back in the pile I isolated a green shirt, compatible socks, and a pair of very old Y-fronts I'd had since leaving school. I dumped them in the hall looking at my watch. If I moved fast I could get there, get them clean, and get out in half an hour. That would give me just less than twenty minutes to change and get into a taxi north. I decided to keep the woollen tube in place and practise walking up the street in it. If I could make it work over two hundred yards there was no reason not to keep it as a standby in case anything should go wrong in the launderette . . .

Concealing my carving knife I hobbled out reflecting on my last visit to a wash-house round the back of the Edgware Road. It was over four years ago, but I swore after that nightmare I would never go into a launderette again. It was the worst one and a half hours of my life. The place was overrun with brats and terrible peroxide mothers. The moment I got through the door I found myself surrounded by brazen punters in whom all grace and etiquette had been routed. They exposed the unwashable. Loaded openly. Dried and folded without pride. Stains didn't interest them. In fact they all seemed determined to show each other just how filthy their families could be . . .

I was in there with about six months-worth. But instead of circulating the building prepared to show everybody what I'd done, I made the serious error of being sensitive about my load. I went in behind a newspaper and dumped into the nearest machine without looking up. My apparent ease at accomplishing what the others were three deep and waiting for gave me a false sense of security – I even asked one of them for change. It was at this point that everything started to go downhill. I couldn't get the money in. After jerking the slide in and out a dozen times I still couldn't get the money in and was forced to ask for assistance. The washer next to me pointed out a sign which said 'Out of Order', and seconds later a one hundred and ninety pound woman came crashing through the crowd shouting, 'Can't you read?' Pensioners and others stood back. I was about to stand back with them when it became clear that it would do no good. She was inflamed enough to fight, and infiltrating into the washers would be useless if she went for me. I smiled at a kid gnawing a bleach bottle instead. Her fury was instantly released into the washing machine. She tried kneeing it open. The resistance angered her, and she stepped back and got into a crouch, and for a moment I thought she was going to have a go at it with her head. Had she, she'd almost certainly have gone through the port-hole and become trapped. It is likely this crossed her mind at the same time it did mine, and thinking better of it, she put a man-stopper into the belly of the machine with her fist. You could tell by the noise she made that this hurt her, but it didn't prevent another punch that would have required an ambu-

lance if delivered in the opposite direction.
Blowing on her knuckles she stood up and
told everybody to keep away because what I
had done was a job for the engineers. We all
agreed with her and she swaggered off, a
path automatically clearing for her to the
telephone where I heard myself described as
a 'Goon' who'd gone and put money into an
'O.O.O.'.

If anything the crowd increased. While we
all waited for the engineers she came back
and I was told to stand off so she could punch
the machine hard enough to lift my packet of
Dreft three inches into the air. A Pensioner
appeared offering to ease the catch with his
screwdriver. I don't know where he got it
from but it was a foot long with a light bulb
in the end. He said he'd been in submarines
and would be able to unscrew the housing.
But the enormous woman didn't want him
anywhere near the housing and she kept her
ground in front of the machine.

23

When the engineers arrived there was only one of them, a Greek, who was more interested in who'd stuck money into an O.O.O. than the O.O.O. itself. The Weight introduced us and I was again asked if I could read.

As soon as the machine was opened I stepped forward to unload, but the vast woman said I'd caused enough trouble and she snatched my bag and got into the hatch herself. Knowledge of what she was in for loosed off a blush. I was reasonably sure nothing so dirty had ever gone into a washing machine, but absolutely certain nothing so filthy had ever come out. As she retracted the first horrible clutch I felt the blood lobbing in my face. Surely, I thought, even she can't be immune? Momentarily she looked at what she had pulled out. Then she said, 'Christ, what's he got in here? I'm not unloading it.' Suddenly the rules were waived. The machine was anybody's. Her idea was that, since I'd put them in, I had to get them out, and I replaced her in a kneeling position in front of the opening. By now every eyeball in the place was involved with what I had, and the air was rich in criticism as my articles came out. Women, who had plunged unspeakable rags into their machines, now took it upon themselves to discuss the comparatively similar items that I transferred into my bag. When I'd finished unloading, I seriously considered crawling to the door. The thought of getting up opposite the Weight filled me with dread: so embarrassed my head throbbed as though she'd hit it. Finally I was forced to stand. Her interest in me was so concentrated I thought I'd have to answer further questions before she'd let me through the door.

'There's one over here?' said the Pensioner, holding a port-hole open.

Now I realised why she wouldn't let him

get at the machine with his screwdriver. The man was obviously of low intelligence. He seriously thought I'd gone through all that, and then could calmly transfer my stuff to the opposite side of the room and go through it all again . . .

'No thank you,' I said. 'I'll come back tomorrow.'

I managed to get outside. It was the first and last time I'd been into a launderette. It had taken me two minutes to fill the machine and an hour and a half waiting in front of it for a man to come from headquarters to rifle the thing open. I was probably the only person in the world to have his washing in a washing machine for one and a half hours without even getting it wet. It was the worst one and a half hours of my life . . .

I was now outside the Speed Queen, Automated Washing Centre, Everything Automatic. It looked like being my lucky day. On my exploratory walk past I noticed

there were only four in there: two Peroxides
(one under hair rollers), one large African,
and one Warden. No visible infants. I came
back and stood outside. Despite a clear
coast and an abundance of free machines
I was reluctant to walk straight in without
going through a rehearsal of my plan.

The building was on a corner. Down its
short side there was a narrow window at
shoulder-height which I thought would be
the best position from which to select my
machine. Looking as inconspicuous as possible, I peered in the window and ran my
eyes up the row. At the far end sticking out
on its own was just what I was after. There
was even an instruction board above it
showing a spiky-haired Goblin with a wand
pointing out what you had to go through.

I silently mouthed myself through the
Goblin's sequence. One: Open the door.
Two: Get the clothes in. Three: Shut the
door (and have three twenty-pence pieces

ready). Four: Put the money in the slot. As I got to five: Push your slot in, a head appeared suddenly at the other side of the window. It came directly between me and my chosen machine, and I said, 'Shove Your Slot In,' straight into her face. It was the big Afro-Caribbean who was taken aback. I think she thought I was a pervert having a look round for underwear. I smiled at her and she disappeared. A moment later the Warden was out on the pavement with her hands on her hips.

'What do you want?' she said.

'It's all right,' I said, 'I'm coming in in a minute.'

'What do you want?'

'I've come to do my washing,' I said, and I showed her my brown-paper bag.

She nodded and went back inside. I could hardly believe it. I had created a bad impression and I was still in the street. I was beginning to wonder if there was something wrong with me. But any hesitation at this point would have sent me home and I walked round to the front of the building and went in before I could analyse my actions. I had clearly been discussed. The one under the rollers covered some brassières with a towel and the West Indian was behind dark glasses.

I did my best to ignore them and made for my machine. As soon as I opened the door and put my stuff in the drum the atmosphere eased a little. I think they were surprised that I was actually in possession of something to wash. My heart was thrashing with concentration to get the sequence right. I was already up to Number Three: Shut the door (and have three twenty-pence pieces ready). Four: Put the money in the slot. Five: Shove your slot in . . .

To my relief there was a rush of water and the thing started spinning. I became almost euphoric. It was all over. All I had to do now

29

was stand in front of it till the things came out clean. I stood back looking casual. With everything under control in the washing section I walked the length of the tiles to have a look at the drying machines. The one under the rollers was in front of hers with half a bagful. I noticed that the technique was to open the door and grab the dry things as they flew past. Obviously this was so more heat could be concentrated into the bulkier items, such as woollens, while at the same time anything fragile, such as bras, would be spared unnecessary exposure. I'd have to remember that for my shirt . . .

Things were going well. My limp was inconspicuous and the spat under control. I walked back past the machines throwing random glances at other people's portholes. A few paces later I found myself back in front of my washing which was still spinning without problem. But it was different to the others. A whole row of machines was washing like mine, but all of them were producing suds which for some reason mine was not. I went over to the Warder and pointed this out.

'Mine hasn't gone white yet,' I said.

'What hasn't?'

'My washing water,' I said, leading her across. She lifted the aluminium flap at the top of the machine.

'You haven't put your soap in,' she said.

'I thought the machines did it by themselves?' She looked at me suspiciously.

'The machine can't put its own soap in. *You* have to put the soap in.'

Her eyes scanned both me and my machine.

'Where is your soap?' she said.

'I haven't got any,' I said. 'It says Everything Automatic?'

'Not soap. Look here. Number Six: Add detergent.'

I looked up at the instruction board. She was right. The Goblin was up there in a crouch over a figure 6 pouring detergent into the hole a figure 6 conveniently forms. I had missed this one behind the African's head.

'What am I going to do?' I said. 'They won't get washed, will they?'

'Not without soap.'

I had done it again. How was it possible for me to keep putting things into washing machines without getting them clean?

The Warder walked away and put on a blue overcoat.

'Look here,' I said, following her into her corner, 'have you got any soap?'

'Soap's in the slot-machine,' she said. 'Ten pence.'

I extracted a small tube of detergent out of the slot-machine and opened my aluminium flap.

'Not now,' said the Warder rushing forward. 'You can't put your soap in now, you've missed your cycle.'

'Have I?'

'You'll have to wait.'

'Will you tell me when to put it in then?'

'No. I'm in a hurry to get home.'

'So am I,' I said.

'You haven't been in here since eight o'clock this morning,' she said.

She put a kind of holeless leather colander on her head and I started to feel insecure.

'What have you got in there?' she said.

'Just socks, and a shirt?'

'Is that all?'

'No.' I paused. 'There's a pair in there as well.'

'A *pair*?'

'Yes.'

'A pair of *pants*?' she repeated, with a hint of indignation. 'Is that all you've put in there?'

'I'm allowed to, aren't I?'

'You can put in a handkerchief for all I care, but I think it's a criminal waste of money.'

'Ha. Ha.' I laughed. 'How right you are. In a weird way, crime's the only reason I'm in here.'

The woman with hair in a blonde smog interrupted her unloading to look up.

'Ha!' I said.

'I'm going home,' said the Warder. 'It's half-past five.'

I looked at my watch. It was in fact ten-past five. But if I'd been in here since eight o'clock this morning, I'd have started lying about a lot more than the time to get out . . .

My anxiety increased. I had missed my cycle. I had neither time nor money for another one. Everybody was at the far end on the drying machines. For some reason I was the only one left at the washing end with a machine that refused to stop spinning. To economise on time I walked

to the back of the building to get my polythene basket ready for when the moment
came. As I passed the pair of Blondes, one of
them said, 'Look out, here he comes.' And
they both instantly ignored each other and
concentrated on their machines. I got hold
of a basket and ignored them. They were
beginning to annoy me, especially the one in
the rollers who looked like Caligula. She
was obviously the ring-leader and determined not to let the matter drop. Every time
I looked up I would contact some suspicious
eye or another, and it was usually one of
hers . . .

Arriving back at my machine, I could
sense she was all set to start stirring it again.
But why? I didn't understand why my ap-
pearance at the window should cause such
interest. I imagined they lived pretty mun-
dane lives in these launderettes, but even
then I couldn't see why a face looking in at a
row of washing machines was anything to

get animated about. One minute later my pilot-light went out and the machine stopped. While opening the hatch, the door to the launderette also opened, and a terrible thing happened. A Beautiful Girl walked in. This was the last thing I wanted. It was bad enough shifting underwear with these louts, but the prospect of doing it with her watching was intolerable. In seconds my spat was out. She didn't notice. The others did. The burnt wool tube around my ankle seemed to justify everything that Caligula had warned them about. This girl was definitely beautiful – a Pakistani with black hair and lots of rings and I didn't see any more. I couldn't look. The combination made me feel fatally ill at ease and try to disguise myself as a regular washer. But my basket looked ridiculous. The others had gone to the back humping loads. I was on my way with two uncleansed dollops. Floor cloths. I was relieved to sling them into a dryer and get in next to Caligula where I hoped her bulk would intercede and the girl wouldn't notice me. Apparently she hadn't. My bewilderment at what she was doing in this hovel was explained when she started feeding coins into the dry-cleaning machine. She had six silk scarves. I felt so unhappy.

The big Afro came rolling over and stood next to me trying to block my view of her drying machine. She obviously didn't like having her stuff on display with the man who'd looked through the window about, and thought she'd stand a better chance of getting home if he was denied any stimulation . . .

Suddenly her door was open. She snatched a brassière in mid-flight and had it down in her sack before I'd even focused on it. The sheer size of the thing dragged my eyes back into her machine to see if there was anything else as big going round. We spotted one at the same time, and out came

37

a harness that may well have had Dunlop written on it.

I got eyes off it but she still deemed it necessary to present me with her massive back. I felt like saying, 'Listen, I don't want to look at your fucking underwear. It may have started fights on the rum farm, but as far as I'm concerned it's about as sexy as a couple of buckets, which is what it looks like.'

I turned my back on her in disgust and found myself face to face with an unrecognisable man in a full-length mirror. He was without eyebrows, eyelashes, and the heat from the oven had given him a kind of crew-cut from mid-forehead across the scalp to the back of the right ear. Short, yellow, ruptured hairs still stuck out, like a Swede's scrotum . . .

'Oh, my God.' And I tried to get my head down. No wonder the Black had a shock when I looked in the window. The sensation

I got was what they'd been talking about for the last half an hour. And they were justified in everything. I looked horrifying. Humphries and his six o'clock appointment were no longer on the agenda. I had to get out of here. And quick.

I was being watched. Caligula had come over and joined the African. I turned sideways and, keeping my back to them, opened the dryer to make a grab for my clothes. The shirt and a sock slapped into my hand, but the pants came over so fast I missed them, and they climbed into the air at speed. I saw them reach their zenith over the hair-rollers and turned away not daring to watch them land. They were lost for ever. I didn't care what happened to them.

A sock was still whizzing insanely behind the glass and I opened the door and went for it. My attempt was unsuccessful and I slammed the hatch. All I wanted to do was get out.

There was a tap on my shoulder.

'Are these yours?'

To my horror the Beautiful Girl was standing there proffering some crisp, but offensive pants . . .

'No,' I growled, giving her the benefit of some shoulder. 'Nothing to do with me.'

'Are they yours?' she asked the African.

'They're *his*,' said Caligula. 'I saw them come out.'

'Excuse me,' said the girl. 'What's your name?'

She smiled very sweetly and I told her.

'Then they are yours,' she said. 'It's embroidered inside on a little tab.'

'Oh yes, those, I never wear them. I lent them to somebody years ago and never seen them since. I don't know how they got in my machine.'

'Don't you want them?'

'Not a lot.'

'I don't want them,' she said.

'Throw them in the bin, love,' said Caligula.

'All right then, I'll take them,' I said, in a somewhat aggressive whisper. 'Thank you, you've been very kind.'

As I snatched the pair my carving knife shot across the floor.

'Look out!' said one of them. 'He's got a blade!'

'Call de cops. Call de cops.'

The one under the rollers was already about it. In a haze of panic I grabbed the knife looking for a friendly face and there wasn't one . . .

'It's not what you think it is. I don't want to hurt anyone.'

They were all backing off.

'I know I look weird, but I'm a writer. I don't normally look like this, and I certainly don't want to use the knife!'

'He's a lunatic.'

'I'm a professional writer for TV.'

Almost simultaneously a fucking siren was going off. She must have got lucky with the patrol car. It must have been virtually outside. I backed off as two Coppers with no laundry crashed through the door. They had hats on and looked enormous. Like giants.

'I'm not in here to hurt anyone,' I said. 'I'm a professional writer.'

'Give me the knife, and you can tell us all about it.'

'Watch him, he's a madman.'

'Give me the knife, and don't give me no mumbo.'

'Mumbo?'

'Mumbo jumbo.'

'I'm innocent,' I said. 'You'll find out. It's not me, it's this bastard in North London.'

'You just come along quietly.'

'They'll get you some help,' said the Beautiful Girl.

'You don't understand. I set fire to myself

42

before I came out. I don't normally look like this.'

'Nice and quiet, now.'

The larger of the constables took the weapon and both took hold of me at an elbow. They had the knife, I had the pants, and with everything still filthy, I was escorted out of the launderette's door . . .